Perfect Crane

Perfect Crane

by Anne Laurin

Illustrated by Charles Mikolaycak

Harper & Row, Publishers

Perfect Crane

Text copyright © 1981 by Anne Laurin

Illustrations copyright © 1981 by Charles Mikolaycak

First Edition

Library of Congress Cataloging in Publication Data
Laurin, Anne.
    Perfect crane.

    SUMMARY: A lonely Japanese magician gains
friends through the paper crane that he brings
to life but then must set free.
    [1. Magicians—Fiction. 2. Cranes (Birds)—
Fiction] I. Mikolaycak, Charles. II. Title.
PZ7.L372794Pe 1980   [E]   80-7912
ISBN 0-06-023743-0
ISBN 0-06-023744-9 (lib. bdg.)

For my mother, who gave me life.
I return still.

NO ONE CAN HOLD THE WIND, or catch the sun, or spin the world like a magician. Some are more powerful than others and some are kinder than others, but none was ever more blessed with magic than Gami.

In painted sandals and printed robes he walked the streets of his town, never speaking to anyone, for he was sure only magicians were interested in magic. And the townsfolk, not knowing what a magician does, never wanted to trouble him. Yet inside, Gami was always troubled.

9

Alone in his house Gami practiced his magic during the day, chanting his charms and spells. But at night he sat silently without a friend to laugh with him or a neighbor to talk to him. Gami's only companions were his hands, busy folding brightly colored paper into flowers and fish and faces. Butterflies of bright blues and reds covered his walls, and delicate birds danced on string in his windows. Gami gave them all his love, for there was no one else.

One dark night Gami folded a speckled red paper into a lily. "Bright flower," he said, "won't you bloom for me and cheer this dreary night?" And then, because Gami *was* a magician, the tiny flower opened its petals right in his hand. Gami was astonished. He had worked much magic, but he had never breathed life into his paper before. He was truly pleased.

The following night Gami folded a lantern of heavy green paper. "Lovely lantern," Gami said, "won't you glow and brighten my tiny house?" And then, because Gami *was* a magician, the lantern dazzled. Gami was so delighted that he did not sleep all night.

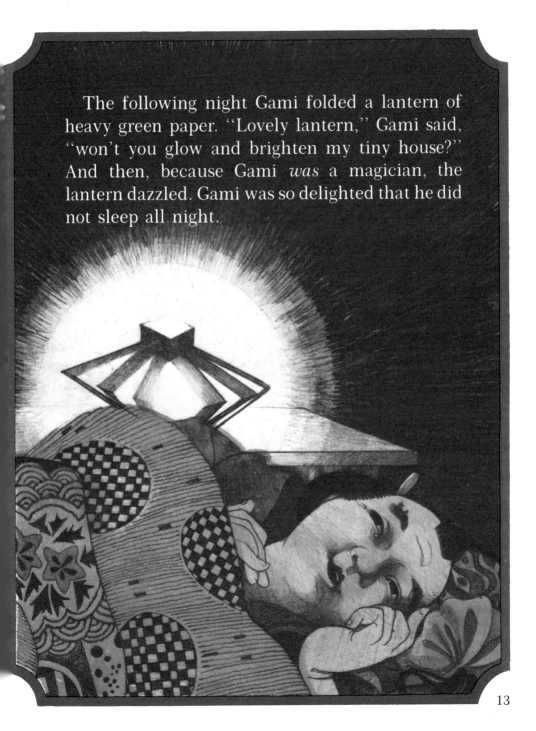

When the day came Gami went directly to the market and bought the finest rice paper, in the purest white. He rolled it carefully and slipped it up his sleeve for safekeeping. Gami had special plans.

That night Gami unrolled his purest-white paper and began folding a crane. He had folded cranes before, with upward wings and lowered heads, but this crane had to be the most perfect. He spent many hours carefully creasing the paper, until at last he set the finished paper bird on the floor.

Gami admired the bird and thought it was the most beautiful he had ever seen. And beyond a doubt, it was. "I have made a flower bloom and a lantern glow," said Gami. "Perfect crane, won't you too come to life for me so I will not be alone anymore?"

15

Slowly the crane rose off the floor and flew up until it was no longer made of paper. It was a real crane. Gami held out his arm and the crane landed gently on it. "You are my father," the crane said. "You have given me life and I am grateful." Gami was filled with joy, knowing he would never be alone again.

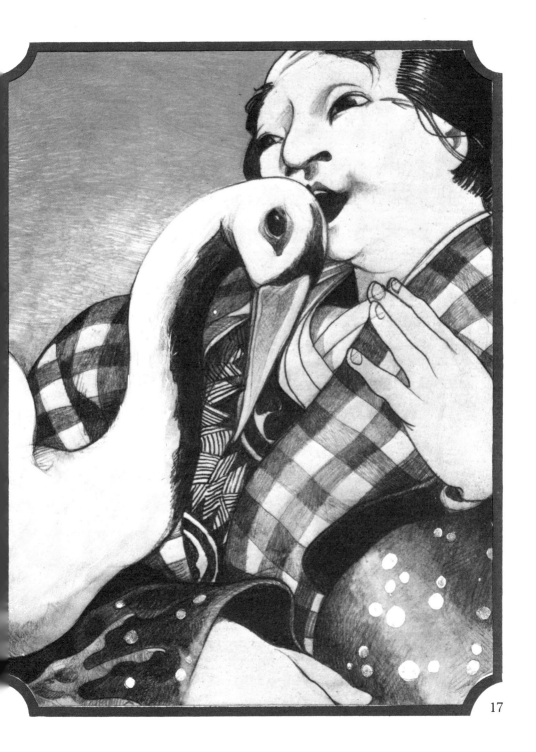

Every day Gami and his crane traveled the town. People looked out of their windows and stopped what they were doing to stare, and soon they could no longer keep quiet.

"Where did you find such a bird?" one man called out to Gami. "For I have truly seen no other like it."

"There *is* no other like it," Gami answered.

"Magician," a woman asked, "how do you get

such a bird to follow you, to live in your house?"

"With my magic," answered Gami. He smiled and would say no more.

"Curious, that magician," his neighbors said. "He is cleverer than we ever guessed." And they came to Gami's house one by one to see the bird and to speak with the magician. The crane gracefully balanced on one leg as Gami talked and joked with his neighbors through the hours of the days.

Then after many months, when the sunlight began to grow weaker and the breeze colder, the crane perched on Gami's windowsill and said, "It is time for me to go."

"What do you mean?" Gami asked. "We have nowhere to go."

"I must join a flock and fly to follow the sun. It is time," said the crane.

"You have given me happiness," Gami said quickly. "Together we have found our friends around us. You cannot leave me."

"You have given me life," the crane said, "but I cannot stay."

Gami lowered his head and began to cry. "I made you," he said, "and now you are going to leave me alone again. I will make you stay."

"Then you will have to return me to paper," the crane said. "A paper bird does not fly and does not need to follow the sun. But a real bird must. There is no other way."

Gami looked at the perfect white crane. He did not want a paper bird and he did not want his perfect crane to fly away.

"Father," the crane said, "I will return in the spring with many stories to tell you. And you will have much to tell me."

Gami was silent. He did not think he would have much to tell if the crane left him. But he knew he had no choice. He had to let his crane go.

And yet, after the crane had joined a flock and flown away, Gami was not left alone. His neighbors, who had first come to see the bird, still came to be with him. They shared their meals and warmed the chilly winter hours with friendly talk. Gami listened to his neighbors, and with his magic he would help if he could. Soon his days and nights were filled with the puzzles and problems of this friend or that.

"Seek the magician," people now said to one another, "whenever you need a friend." And Gami was always glad to lend a hand or a heart.

For many months Gami was so busy that he did not notice the small sprigs of grass or the buds on the trees. He did not notice spring.

Then one day as the new sun filled Gami's house, a shadow crossed his window and he looked up to see the perfect crane land on the sill. Gami rushed to the window, and when he reached the crane he stopped and bowed his head in thanks.

"You have returned," Gami said at last.

"As I always will," the crane answered. "And I have so much to tell you." The crane described a faraway port where small boats bob on salty green water. "I have spent nights by swiftly running rivers and found harvested winter fields with loose grain to eat. I have come to know many places, Father."

"That is good," said Gami. "I have come to know many people. Old Miki down the hill lost all his chickens save one. I shed a spell on her so that every egg she lays is twins." Gami smiled with delight and the crane nodded his head in approval.

"And surely you remember that small boy, that sick boy who can only sit in a chair at his door. For

him," Gami said proudly, "I folded out of fine sturdy paper a kite without string, a bird without wings. It is a toy never seen before that he sails through the air and that always returns to land in his lap. Children gather from all around to watch, but the toy works only for him. I was surely pleased with that!"

"Come, there is much to show you," Gami said, and together they went out into the streets of the town. People stopped them to greet the bird and to give thanks that he had returned to their friend. And some people stopped them just because they needed Gami's help, for now everyone knew the good work of the magician.

While the blossoms on the trees turned to fruit in the sun, Gami and his crane spent long days in the streets and the markets and the houses of good friends. And when the summer months had passed and the fruit was taken and stored away, the crane was ready to go once again. Gami did not worry as he and his neighbors stood at the door and wished the crane farewell. He knew his crane would return with the spring, and the crane still returns to this very day. For perfect cranes have the blessings of magicians and live for all time.

Design by Charles Mikolaycak and Ellen Weiss
Set in 14/17 Primer,
with display in Mistral
Composed by Cardinal Type Service, Inc.
Printed by Rae Publishing Company, Inc.
Bound by The Book Press
Harper & Row, Publishers, Inc.